The Creek

Farmers of the Southeast

by Tracey Boraas

Capstone
press

Mankato, Minnesota

Capstone Press
151 Good Counsel Drive, P.O. Box 669, Mankato, Minnesota 56002.
www.capstonepress.com

Library of Congress Cataloging-in-Publication Data
Boraas, Tracey.
     The Creek: Farmers of the Southeast/by Tracey Boraas.
          v. cm. — (American Indian nations)
     Includes bibliographical references and index.
     Contents: Who are the Creek?—Traditional life—Conflict and
change—A new place and way of life—The Creek today.
     ISBN 0-7368-1566-X (hardcover)
     ISBN 0-7368-4823-1 (paperback)
     1. Creek Indians—Juvenile literature. [1. Creek Indians.
2. Indians of North America—Southern States.] I. Title.
II. American Indian nations series.
E99.C9 B67 2003
975.004'973—dc21   2002012936

Summary: An overview of the past and present of the Creek people. Traces
their customs, family life, history, and culture, as well as relations with the
U.S. government.

Editorial Credits
Charles Pederson, editor; Kia Adams, designer; Alta Schaffer, photo
researcher; Karen Risch, product planning editor

Photo Credits
Capstone Press/Gary Sundermeyer, 15
Corbis, 12, 35; Richard A. Cooke, 8–9; Bettmann, 20–21; Underwood &
     Underwood, 36; Werner Forman, 44
Kit Breen, cover (inset), 4, 38, 41, 42
Muscogee (Creek) Nation, 40
National Archives and Records Administration, 33
North Wind Picture Archives, cover (main), 11, 22, 26
PhotoDisc, Inc., 14–15
Phyllis Fife, 18
Stock Montage, Inc., 17, 25, 29
The University Museum, University of Arkansas, 37, 45
Woolaroc Museum, Bartlesville, OK/Robert Lindneux, 30–31

1 2 3 4 5 6 08 07 06 05 04 03

**The publisher wishes to thank Pamela S. Wallace, Ph.D., for her help in
preparing this book.**

Table of Contents

Features

Some Creek people take part in powwows with other American Indian nations. More than 52,000 people consider themselves part of the Creek people.

Chapter One

Who Are the Creek?

The Creek people are an American Indian nation. The 2000 U.S. Census shows that 40,223 people identify themselves as Creek. The Creek themselves count more than 52,000 people as Creek.

The largest Creek group in the United States is the Muscogee (Creek) Nation. Most of these Creek live in eastern Oklahoma farms and towns. Their headquarters is in Okmulgee, Oklahoma. In the early 1800s, these Creek were forced to move from Georgia and Alabama to Oklahoma.

Smaller Creek groups are located in Oklahoma and other states. One of these groups is the Poarch Band Creek. The Poarch Band lives in Alabama, where the Creek culture first developed.

The "Creek"

English traders in what became South Carolina were the first people to use the Creek name. They used the word because the Indians they first met lived along creeks.

The English considered the local groups one nation. The groups saw themselves as separate parts of a loose partnership. This alliance probably began for protection from larger tribes to the north.

Many tribes made up the alliance. Alliance tribes may have spoken as many as six different languages. Most tribes spoke one of the Muskogean languages.

After the Revolutionary War (1775–1783) ended, the government of the United States began calling the alliance the Creek Confederacy. All the people in it were called Creek. Today, many Creek people call themselves "Muscogee."

Most confederacy tribes shared similar traditions. They built towns where everyone was responsible for the group's survival. Their spiritual life was based on respect for nature and family. These traditions helped the Creek when they were forced to move from their southeastern homeland to the Indian Territory. Indian Territory later became the state of Oklahoma.

Modern Creek celebrate their rich history. They live much like other Americans. But even so, they continue to practice Creek ways of life including traditional food, clothing, games, and other customs.

UNITED STATES

OKLAHOMA

* HORSESHOE BEND

ALABAMA   GEORGIA   *ATLANTIC OCEAN*

* FORT MIMS

Gulf of Mexico

Scale
Miles
0   250   500
0   250   500
Kilometers

Legend
Creek Lands about 1800
Modern Creek Lands
Modern United States
Other Countries
* Battle Site

The snake-shaped Serpent Mound in Ohio is a reminder of the Hopewell culture. The Creek are descended from this ancient culture.

Chapter Two

Traditional Life

No one knows exactly how the Creek culture developed. Archeologists, who study past cultures, believe Creek culture began with the Adenas about 3,000 years ago. The Hopewell culture of 300 B.C. to A.D. 600 continued the Adena culture. Both groups lived along coasts and rivers in what became Ohio, Illinois, West Virginia, Louisiana, Alabama, Georgia, and Florida.

The Mississippian culture came from the Hopewell and Adena cultures. Around the year 600, the Mississippians lived along many river valleys of the Mississippi River system. By 800, they had spread throughout the South and East. Mississippians grew corn, beans, squash, and other vegetables in the rich river valleys.

Like the Adena and Hopewell, the Mississippians built large mounds. Some were used as burial mounds. The Mississippians also placed temples and chiefs' homes on the mounds. An average mound was about 30 feet (9 meters) high and 250 feet (76 meters) around. Some mounds were as large as 75 feet (23 meters) high and 600 feet (183 meters) around.

The Mississippians built the mounds without using animals or machines. They probably carried one basket of dirt at a time to the construction site. Hundreds of workers needed several years to build a mound.

In 1539, Spanish explorer Hernando de Soto led an army through the Southeast to look for gold. While searching, he met Mississippians. He forced some of them into slavery and fought others. The Mississippians caught measles, smallpox, and other deadly diseases from the Spanish. The Mississippians did not have medicine to fight the diseases. Many people became ill and died. Their culture began to disappear.

The Beginnings of the Modern Creek

As the Mississippian culture disappeared, groups survived with new ways of life. They joined to form small settlements. They built farm communities in river valleys and along streams with loose, rich soil. These people became the modern Creek.

Creek families lived on rectangular areas of gardens and fields. Each family plot had one or more houses. The houses served different purposes. Summer houses were built to be cool. Four poles supported a platform and a roof of leaves and grass. These houses provided shade from the sun's heat.

Hernando de Soto, right, led Spanish explorers through the Southeast in search of gold. He did not find gold, but he did meet American Indians.

Winter houses were built to be warm. The Creek wove thin tree branches between large posts. They then spread a mixture of clay and grass over the branches to make walls. Roofs were made of cypress tree bark. Winter homes had a central fireplace that also served as a kitchen.

Later, the Creek learned from Europeans to build log cabins. In the 1700s, the Creek used log cabins for both winter and summer shelter.

In the 1700s, the Creek built log cabins for shelter.

Creek Towns

The Creek lived in large towns and small villages. In each large town, family plots surrounded a central open area. The Creek used the area for dances, religious ceremonies, and games. The open area also contained a council house. Some council houses could hold as many as 500 people.

In the Creek Confederacy, each town or village had its own leaders. Each town had a chief and an assistant chief. The chief used a messenger to announce decisions to the people. Chiefs from confederacy towns met together to discuss problems affecting all Creek.

Towns in the confederacy were called red or white towns. Red towns were war towns. Whenever the Creek went to war, leaders from red towns met to choose a war chief. White towns were known as peace towns. After a war ended, peace talks took place in a white town. A Creek council invited defeated tribes to join the confederacy.

During hundreds of years, the Creek population grew. By the early 1800s, the Creek Confederacy had 44 towns and 18,000 to 22,000 people.

When a Creek town reached a population of about 400 to 600 people, it split. About half the people moved to a nearby site and started a new town. They called their old towns "mother towns" and the new ones "daughter towns." Mother and daughter towns cooperated closely with each other.

Village Roles

Women and children had important roles in Creek towns. Creek women were the heads of families and owned the property. Women and children worked large garden plots shared among the townspeople. Each family also worked a smaller garden of its own. The women and children used digging sticks and sharp stones or bones to hoe the soil. Women and children gathered herbs, roots, nuts, berries, and wild rice for food. They gathered special plants for medicines. They prepared meals and made clothing, pottery, and baskets.

Men fished to provide food for the village. They sometimes used spears or bows and arrows to catch fish. The fishers sometimes made a fish poison from a root called devil's shoestring. They pounded the root into a powder and sprinkled it on the water. The poison killed the fish but did not harm people. When the dead fish floated to the surface of the water, the men could scoop them up and prepare them for eating.

Men also provided meat for the village by hunting. They made long hunting journeys lasting nearly six months. The hunters brought home deer, bear, turkey, rabbit, and squirrel. The meat was dried or smoked to last throughout the year. The Creek always shared their food with those who needed it.

Muskogean Shuckbread

The Creek considered corn a holy food. In midsummer, they celebrated the ripening of the corn.

   To make shuckbread, the Creek wrapped corn leaves, or cornshucks, around a cornmeal mixture. Shuckbread is served as a side dish with meals. Ask an adult to help you with the recipe.

Ingredients
4 cups (960 mL) water
cornshucks from four ears of corn
2 cups (480 mL) cornmeal
1 teaspoon (5 mL) salt
about 1½ cups (360 mL) water
maple syrup

Equipment
large saucepan with lid
wooden mixing spoon
large mixing bowl

What You Do

1. In large saucepan, bring water to a boil.
2. Boil cornshucks for 10 minutes. With the mixing spoon, remove them from water and set aside to cool. Save water for step 6.
3. In large bowl, mix cornmeal and salt. Add as much water as needed to form a stiff mixture.
4. With your hands, form cornmeal mixture into four equal balls.
5. Completely wrap each ball in boiled cornshucks.
6. Drop wrapped balls into the previously boiled water.
7. Cover saucepan. Cook at low heat for 1 hour.
8. With spoon, remove from water. Let water drain from balls and remove from cornshucks. Serve warm with maple syrup.

Serves 4

Family Life

Large family groups called clans were the center of Creek communities. The people in the clan were related. Children were members of their mothers' clans. Clans were named after the wind and after wolves, panthers, skunks, alligators, and other animals. Clan members might live in several different towns and villages.

By age 3 or 4, children began to learn their place as a Creek person. Unclothed until this age, children began to dress according to custom. Boys began to wear a breechcloth, a piece of cloth that hung from the waist in the front and back. Girls began to wear skirts of deerskin leather or of woven plants.

Adults taught the children what they needed to know. A mother's oldest brother taught her boys how to live as Creeks and become leaders and hunters. The mother's oldest sister taught the girls. Boys and girls learned to respect elders and to pay attention to spiritual matters. They also learned clan histories and tribal histories.

Creek marriage was not complicated. When a Creek man wanted to marry, he offered gifts of furs and meat to the woman's family. If the family accepted the gifts and the woman agreed, the man moved in with his wife and her clan relatives. The marriage was recognized during a yearly celebration called the Green Corn Ceremony. Men and women from the same clan did not marry each other.

Traditional Creek clothing was made of leather and furs like that worn by other Native American tribes.

The Origin of the Clans

The Creek tell a story about the earliest people and how they formed clans. The Creek say that at the beginning of time, their people came from a hole in the ground. The Creator covered Earth with a thick fog that blinded the people. They wandered in small groups searching for food. Animals traveled with each group to guide them through the fog.

At last, the Creator sent a wind to blow away the fog. The people finally could see again. To honor the wind, one group of Creek called themselves the Wind Clan. Other groups took the name of the animal that guided them. The Creator told the Creek they were the first people of their clans and must bring honor to their clan names.

Religion

The Creek have always been spiritual people. They believed corn, fire, and many animals were sacred. The Creek believed good and bad spirits brought sickness and health.

The medicine maker was the most important Creek religious leader. To heal the sick, he sang special songs and used medicines made of plants. He taught religious ceremonies.

Hunters practiced religious ceremonies. Before going on long hunts, hunters cleansed themselves by fasting and vomiting. If hunters killed an animal, they thanked it for the food it provided.

The Green Corn Ceremony was an important Creek religious ceremony. For several days in the middle of the summer, the Creek celebrated health, happiness, friendship, and the ripening corn. At the start of the festival, men drank asi. They believed this strong black tea cleansed their bodies and spirits. Feasting, dancing, singing, and storytelling followed the cleansing. During the Green Corn Ceremony, crimes were forgiven, friendships were renewed, and new members were adopted into towns.

Spanish people settled in Saint Augustine in Florida in the 1600s. From Saint Augustine and other Florida towns, settlers and missionaries pushed north into Creek land.

Chapter Three

Conflict and Change

The Creek established themselves in two main areas. The Lower Creek lived between the Chattahoochee and Flint Rivers in present-day Georgia. The Upper Creek lived between the Coosa and Tallapoosa Rivers in present-day Alabama. For more than 100 years after Hernando de Soto's visit, few Europeans had contact with the Creek in these areas.

During the 1600s and 1700s, many Europeans moved closer to the Creek from all sides. Spanish explorers and religious missionaries moved north from Florida. English settlers pushed west from the Atlantic Coast. French trappers traveled down the Mississippi River from Canada and advanced east. These European groups wanted to control Indian land, wealth, or trading networks. Europeans gave Indian leaders gifts to win their friendship. Many Indians sided with one European group or another.

Trade Brings Power to the Creek

In 1670, the English built a settlement called Charles Town in the colony of Carolina. English traders traveled to Creek towns along a river they called Ochese Creek. They named the Indians along this river the Ochese Creek Indians. Soon, the

Charles Town, Carolina, was a busy shipping port in the 1700s. Traders traveled from the town to trade with the Creek. Charles Town later became known as Charleston, South Carolina.

English dropped the word Ochese and called all the Indians Creek.

Trade with the English changed how the Lower Creek lived. English traders gave the Lower Creek guns, bullets, cloth, metal tools, and other goods in exchange for furs and prisoners. The guns allowed the Creek to hunt animals more easily and to fight against other tribes. The English traders shipped the skins to England. They sold the prisoners as slaves to work on English farms.

The Lower Creek became the most powerful people in the Southeast. But English products replaced Creek products. The Creek became dependent on English goods.

In 1717, the Georgia colonial government made Indian slavery illegal. The Creek ended their slave trade but continued to trade deerskins for English goods. Creek hunters killed between 45,000 and 50,000 deer each year.

Many Creek began to adopt European ways. They used plows and raised farm animals. Some people built log homes. Some Creek married Europeans and dressed like them. A few Creek owned large farms called plantations. Some Creek owned hundreds of African American slaves and thousands of cattle. The Creek became known as one of the Five Civilized Tribes of the Southeast.

The French and Indian War

A desire for land led to the French and Indian War (1754–1763). France and Great Britain wanted land for fur trade. American Indians often fought for one side or the other. The Creek fought on the side of the British.

After nine years, Great Britain won the war. Parts of Florida and land east of the Mississippi River came under British control.

At the war's end, the Creek occupied 84,000 square miles (217,560 square kilometers). Great Britain thought the Creek would be helpful allies if fights to control North America continued. The British gave them more guns, bullets, and farm equipment. To protect Creek land, Great Britain made it against the law for British and Americans to settle west of the Appalachian Mountains.

Trying to Save Their Land

British colonists in North America ignored the law and moved onto Indian land. This movement caused trouble between the British government and their colonists in America. Troubles finally led to the U.S. Revolutionary War. The Creek sided with the British, but the Americans won the war. Power shifted from Great Britain to the United States.

Respected Creek leader Alexander McGillivray thought of a way to protect Creek land from Americans. He wrote to the British and Spanish governments, which still controlled parts of North America. He asked them to recognize the Creek Confederacy as an independent nation. That way, he hoped the U.S. government also would have to treat the Creek like any independent country.

McGillivray's efforts caught the attention of U.S. President Thomas Jefferson. Jefferson supported a law to protect Indian

Many Creek leaders wanted to protect Creek land from the Americans. The leader pictured here was named Opothle Yoholo.

Alexander McGillivray

Alexander McGillivray was an important Creek leader during the Revolutionary War. His exact birthdate is unknown. He probably was born in 1759 near present-day Montgomery, Alabama. His father was from Scotland. His mother was half Creek and half French.

McGillivray believed the Americans would threaten Indian land if they gained independence from Great Britain. He urged the Creek to stay loyal to the British during the Revolutionary War.

After the war, McGillivray tried to protect Creek land from settlers. As part of his plan, he worked to unite the Creek under a central government. He believed the Creek could best protect their lands by using the political system of the white people.

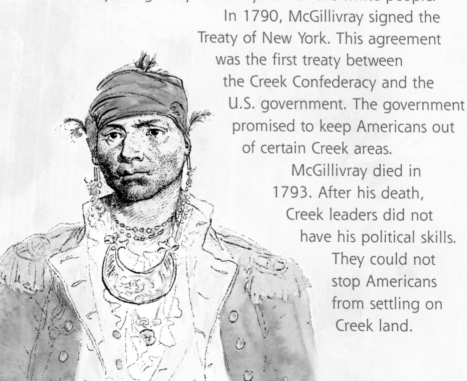

In 1790, McGillivray signed the Treaty of New York. This agreement was the first treaty between the Creek Confederacy and the U.S. government. The government promised to keep Americans out of certain Creek areas.

McGillivray died in 1793. After his death, Creek leaders did not have his political skills. They could not stop Americans from settling on Creek land.

land. This law said the United States would never take land from Indians unless they agreed.

The Red Stick War

After McGillivray died in 1793, the Creek Confederacy broke into groups. The groups disagreed about dealing with the U.S. government. A group of Upper Creek called Red Sticks wanted to keep their traditions and fight the white people. Another group argued the Creek could survive only if they adopted white people's ways.

White people wanted the valuable Creek land for farming and mining. To get it, they attacked Creek towns. In 1811, the U.S. government built a road through Creek territory. Settlers used the road to move quickly but illegally onto Creek land.

Red Stick warriors started attacking white settlements for revenge. Frightened settlers moved to forts for protection.

The Creek began to fight each other. Many chiefs did not want war with the United States. They killed warriors who fought against white settlers.

Fights went on between settlers and Red Sticks. In 1813, white raiders attacked a Creek village on Burnt Corn Creek, in present-day Alabama. The attack began the Red Stick War (1813–1814). The whites killed any Creek they found. To get back at the whites, Red Sticks attacked Fort Mims, Alabama. They killed most of the soldiers and settlers in the fort.

After the Fort Mims attack, General Andrew Jackson gathered an army to fight the Red Sticks. His forces included militia members, settlers, and people of the Chickasaw, Choctaw, Cherokee, and Lower Creek. Jackson's group marched across Creek territory, burning Red Stick villages.

The last fight of the Red Stick War was the Battle of Horseshoe Bend. On March 27, 1814, Jackson's fighters trapped the Upper Creek Red Sticks at a bend in the Tallapoosa River in Alabama. More than 600 warriors died. The Red Sticks lost the war.

The Creek Lose Their Homeland

The treaty that followed the Battle of Horseshoe Bend gave about half the Creek land in Alabama to the United States. The U.S. government promised the Creek could keep their land in western Georgia.

In 1825, William McIntosh and 12 other Creek leaders discussed another treaty with U.S. Indian agents. McIntosh and the chiefs sold the remaining Creek land to the United States. For his help, the U.S. government paid McIntosh $25,000.

Creek law did not allow the sale of tribal land without the approval of all Creek leaders. McIntosh and the 12 other leaders had broken this law. The Creek Council ordered the 13 men to be killed.

In 1829, Andrew Jackson was elected U.S. president. In May 1830, his government passed the Indian Removal Act. The law gave the Creek and other Southeast Indian nations five years to move west to Indian Territory in present-day Oklahoma. Some Lower Creek left immediately. Most Creek stayed. Even before the Creek had left, settlers started occupying their land.

William McIntosh was one of several Creek leaders who sold Creek land to the U.S. government. The Creek Council ordered the men to be killed.

The Indian Removal Act forced many American Indians to move west. The Creek experienced harsh conditions during removal.

Chapter Four

A New Place and Way of Life

In 1836, the official Creek removal to the Indian Territory started. At the start of removal, the Creek numbered more than 21,000 people. A few Upper Creek escaped to southern Alabama and northern Florida. Other Creek refused to move and were arrested by the U.S. Army.

During removal, the Creek traveled by different means. Some were crowded onto small boats that floated down the Alabama River and across the Gulf of Mexico. They then traveled up the Mississippi River to the Arkansas Territory. The last part of the journey to Oklahoma was by land. Other Creek were forced to make the entire march by land.

Conditions were terrible. Many Creek wore light clothing. Some walked without shoes along cold, muddy trails and hard, frozen paths. Diseases spread easily among the weakened people. As many as 3,500 Creek died making their way to Oklahoma. By the end of 1837, the U.S. government reported that the Creek removal was complete.

Settling in Indian Territory

The Lower Creek who had left in 1830 had rebuilt their lives in the West. Many were unhappy to have 15,000 Upper Creek entering their land in 1836.

The Upper Creek rebuilt traditional Creek towns and continued ceremonial life and government. Some of them settled with family and friends already on the Arkansas River. Most settled in the southwestern part of Creek land along the Canadian River. These Creek shared their goods so everyone could survive.

The Lower Creek adopted the settlers' style of dress, the Christian religion, and the American education system. They lived on family farms and owned slaves. Some of these Lower Creek did not share with each other or their Upper Creek neighbors.

The Upper and Lower Creek sent representatives to tribal councils. In 1840, they united under one National Council. Each town picked its own leaders as part of the council.

Christianity and Education

The Lower Creek were open to the teachings of Christian religious teachers. Many Creek believed their children must learn to read to succeed in the world. They wanted Christian teachers to come and teach Creek children.

Many Upper Creek leaders were against non-Creek religions. The National Council agreed and did not allow Christianity on the Creek Reservation. Any Creek who taught the Christian religion or attended a Christian church was whipped.

In 1841, the council finally agreed to let a Christian group called Presbyterians build a school on the Creek Reservation. In 1843, the first of several Christian boarding schools for

Holding Sunday School classes was one way Christians spread their beliefs among the Creek. The children above were photographed in the 1920s.

Creek opened. Many Creek children lived at these schools. They learned English and were not allowed to speak their own language. They could not practice Creek traditions. They were encouraged to live like white Americans.

War and Rebuilding

Under the National Council, the Creek were united. A written constitution was nearly complete. Then, the Civil War (1861–1865) began.

The war split the Creek again. Creek slave owners chose to fight for the Southern states. Other Creek fought for the Northern states.

Fighting spread through Indian Territory. Soldiers from both the North and South burned Creek towns and farms. They killed livestock and destroyed fields.

By the end of the war, the Creek had nothing left but their land. The U.S. government took much of that land to resettle other Indian nations from the Great Plains. Once again, the Creek had to rebuild their lives.

In 1867, the Creek adopted a form of government similar to that of the United States. Instead of a president, the Creek had a principal chief. The National Council was like the U.S. Congress. It was made up of the House of Kings and the House of Warriors. The Creek also created a system of judges.

Allotments and the End of Indian Territory

In 1887, the U.S. government passed the General Allotment Act. This law divided reservations in Indian Territory into 160-acre (65-hectare) farms. Each Creek person received one farm, or allotment. The U.S. government sold any tribal land left over from the allotments to white settlers.

Allotments changed Creek life. The Creek lost much of their tribal land. They had to end the practice of using their

Members of the Creek government met at the Council House in about 1880.

land for the good of all Creek. They had little experience owning land. Dishonest people cheated thousands of Creek and other Oklahoma Indians out of their allotments. A few Creek discovered oil fields on their land and became rich. The government did not allow the Creek to choose their own chiefs. Instead, the U.S. government chose chiefs for them.

In November 1907, Oklahoma became a state. Indian Territory and the Five Civilized Tribes no longer existed.

Regaining Their Independence

In 1936, Congress passed the Oklahoma Indian Welfare Act. This law helped the Oklahoma Creek regain some of their tribal lands. The law helped revive the Creek Nation.

In the early 1900s, oil fields were discovered on Creek land. The oil made some Creek wealthy.

Chunkey

In the early 1900s, the Creek were not allowed to practice their traditions, including some games. Chunkey is a Creek game for two players. The game dates back to the Mississippian culture.

To play, players roll a special smooth, round stone about 5 to 6 inches (13 to 15 centimeters) wide along the ground. Each player throws a long, slender pole at the stone. The thrower who hits the stone or gets closest to it scores a point.

Traditionally, chunkey games took a great deal of preparation. A town might play only one game a year. Today, the Creek sometimes play chunkey at yearly festivals.

Other steps to independence took place. In 1968, the U.S. government returned Oklahoma lands to the Creek. In 1969, the government paid $4 million for land it took from the Creek in the 1800s. To claim a share of this money, people had to prove they were descendants of the original Creek. In 1971, the Creek regained the right to elect their principal chief.

A small number of Creek have rebuilt their culture in southern Alabama. They belong to the Poarch Band Creek near Poarch, Alabama. They are descended from the Creek who stayed in Georgia and Alabama in the 1830s. In 1939, Alabama started to provide elementary schools for the Poarch Band Creek. Finally, in 1950, Alabama allowed Poarch students to attend high school with other students. Today, the Poarch Creek govern themselves on their own reservation.

Powwow dancing is a modern Creek activity. Older Creek pass on their history and traditions to younger generations.

Chapter Five

The Creek Today

Today's Creek are U.S. citizens with a special history they want to remember. Older Creek pass on Creek traditions to younger Creek. These traditions include dancing and learning the Creek language.

The Creek Nation in Oklahoma and the Poarch Band Creek in Alabama have tribal governments to develop programs for better education, health care, and jobs. Tribal government helps provide housing for Creek with low incomes.

The Muscogee (Creek) Nation of Oklahoma elects a principal chief and

Chief Robert Perry Beaver

Chief Robert Perry Beaver is the Principal Chief of the Creek Nation. He grew up on his grandmother's farm near Morris, Oklahoma. He graduated from Morris High School. Chief Beaver then attended Northeast Louisiana State University, earning a bachelor of science degree in mathematics. He earned a master's degree in education from Central State University in Edmond, Oklahoma.

Chief Beaver had a successful athletic and education career. During the 1960s, he played football for the Green Bay Packers. He spent 25 years as head football coach at Jenks High School in Jenks, Oklahoma. As head coach, he led two teams to state championships. Chief Beaver also served as the high school's Indian Education Director. In 1991, he retired from education.

Chief Beaver has earned several sports awards. He belongs to the Oklahoma High School Coaches Hall of Fame. In 1998, he was elected to the Northeast Louisiana State University Hall of Fame. In 2000, he was elected to the American Indian Athletic Hall of Fame.

Since then, Chief Beaver has been active in the Creek Nation's government. He served twice as the Creek second chief. In January 1996, he was elected principal chief. He is the third principal chief elected since 1971, the year the Creek Nation regained the right to elect its own leaders.

Chief Beaver and his wife, Mariam Bruner Beaver, live in Jenks, Oklahoma. They have four grown children.

second chief. These chiefs are similar to state governors. The 26-member National Council makes laws for the nation. The Creek Nation's court system decides cases about tribal laws.

The Creek Nation of Oklahoma and the Poarch Band Creek in Alabama run many successful businesses. These businesses include small stores, travel stops, tobacco shops, bingo halls, hotels, metal factories, and farm-related businesses. The businesses provide jobs for tribal members. The businesses help the Creek earn money to support themselves.

The tribal government of the Muscogee (Creek) Nation is located in Okmulgee, Oklahoma. Creek governments help their people improve their lives.

A monument in Okmulgee, Oklahoma, shows a Creek woman wearing a traditional dress. Creek women today sometimes wear similar dresses. Continuing such traditions has helped the Creek remain strong and united.

Staying Strong

Every summer, the Creek hold special religious festivals at sacred ceremonial centers called stomp grounds. These religious festivals are not open to the public. Many Creek gather at the stomp grounds to listen to stories and advice from respected elders. The Creek join in religious and social dances. They play Creek games of stickball and chunkey. On special days, many Creek gather at their stomp grounds to drink asi. This tea is still used to bring physical and spiritual cleansing.

Finger weaving is another popular tradition that unites the Creek. Creek women use their fingers to weave narrow strips of fabric into decorative belts. They wear the belts with other traditional clothing at ceremonies.

The Creek continue their traditions, which have kept them strong and united. They want to pass along their traditions to future generations of Creek. Taking part in these activities is one way the Creek people celebrate their history and unite them as a nation.

Creek Timeline

The Revolutionary War is fought; the Creek fight for the British.

The Red Stick War is fought.

| 1539 | 1775–1783 | 1790 | 1813–1814 |

Hernando de Soto leads his army through the Southeast.

The Treaty of New York becomes the first treaty between the United States and the Creek Confederacy.

Hopewell people created this copper figure of a crow.

The U.S. government passes the Indian Removal Act.

The U.S. government pays the Creek $4 million for land it took away in the Southeast.

| 1830 | 1887 | 1969 | 1971 |

The Creek regain the right to choose their own chiefs.

Congress passes the General Allotment Act to split up reservations into smaller pieces of land.

Glossary

allotment (uh-LOT-muhnt)—a plot of land that American Indians received when the U.S. government divided tribal land

Christianity (kriss-chee-AN-uh-tee)—a religion based on the life and teachings of Jesus Christ

clan (KLAN)—a large group of related families

confederacy (kuhn-FED-ur-uh-see)—a union of towns or tribes with a common goal

Indian Territory (IN-dee-uhn TER-uh-tor-ee)—land where the U.S. government forced many American Indians to move in the 1800s; Indian Territory later became Oklahoma.

sacred (SAY-krid)—holy, highly valued, or important

tradition (truh-DISH-uhn)—a custom, idea, or belief handed down from one generation to the next

Internet Sites

Track down many sites about the Creek. Visit the FACT HOUND at *http://www.facthound.com.* IT IS EASY! IT IS FUN!

1) Go to *http://www.facthound.com*
2) Type in: 073681566X
3) Click on "FETCH IT," and FACT HOUND will find several links hand-picked by our editors.

Relax and let our pal FACT HOUND do the research for you!

Places to Write and Visit

Creek Council House Museum
106 West Sixth Street
Okmulgee, OK 74447

Horseshoe Bend National Military Park
11288 Horseshoe Bend Road
Daviston, AL 36256-9751

Muscogee (Creek) Nation Complex
1801 East Fourth Street
Okmulgee, OK 74447-3901

For Further Reading

Ansary, Mir Tamim. *Southeast Indians.* Native Americans. Des Plaines, Ill.: Heinemann Library, 2000.

Feinstein, Stephen. *Andrew Jackson.* Presidents. Berkeley Heights, N.J.: MyReportLinks.comBook, 2002.

Gray-Kanatiiosh, Barbara A. *The Creek.* Native Americans. Edina, Minn.: Abdo, 2002.

Nardo, Don. *The Relocation of the North American Indian.* History of the World. San Diego: KidHaven Press, 2002.

Index